marisabina russo

Mama talks too much

Greenwillow Books New York

For Thérèse and Corey

Gouache paints were used to prepare the full-color art.
The text type is Geometric 415 Medium BT.

Copyright © 1999 by Marisabina Russo Stark
Printed in Hong Kong by South China Printing Company (1988) Ltd.
First Edition   10 9 8 7 6 5 4 3 2 1

Library of Congress Cataloging-in-Publication Data
Russo, Marisabina.
Mama talks too much / by Marisabina Russo.
p.   cm.
Summary: On the way to the store, Celeste is frustrated when her mother constantly stops
to talk with neighborhood friends, until Celeste finds a reason of her own for stopping.
ISBN 0-688-16411-0
[1. Neighborliness—Fiction.   2. City and town life—Fiction.   3. Mother and child—Fiction.]
I. Title.   PZ7.R9192Mam   1999   [E]—dc21
98-17695   CIP   AC

On Saturday mornings my mama
and I walk to the supermarket.

I pull the folded metal carriage and run ahead as fast as I can. The wheels of the carriage go bump, bump, *BUMP* as they roll across the cracks in the sidewalk.

I run until I hear Mama calling, "Slow down, Celeste! Wait for me!"

Mama walks too slowly. But I wait while she catches up. At the corner she takes my hand, even though I think I'm big enough to cross the street by myself.

Then we see Mrs. Green and I say, "Oh no!"

Mama stops.

Mrs. Green stops.

Now I have to stop.

"How are you?"

"I haven't seen you in ages!"

"What's new?"

They talk and talk and talk.

Blah, blah, blah.

I watch the cars go by.
I count the red ones.
I count the white ones.
And then I tug at Mama's arm.
"Let's go," I say.

"Nice seeing you," says Mama.

"Call me!" says Mrs. Green.

At last we're on our way again.

Past the shoe repair,

past the Laundromat,

past the drugstore.

Then we see Mrs. Walker and I say, "Oh no!"

Mama stops.

Mrs. Walker stops.

Now I have to stop.

"I've been meaning to call you!"

"I've been sick all week."

"I'm so sorry to hear that."

They talk and talk and talk.

Blah, blah, blah.

I count the rings on Mrs. Walker's fingers.

I count the chains around her neck.

I count the bracelets around her wrist.

And then I tug at Mama's pocketbook.

"Come on, Mama," I say.

"I'll call you," says Mama.

"Don't forget!" says Mrs. Walker.

At last we're on our way again.

Past the fruit stand,

past the bakery,

past the newsstand.

Then we see Mr. Chan and I say, "Oh no!"

Mama stops.

Mr. Chan stops.

Now I have to stop.

"I didn't see you at the tenants' meeting."

"What did I miss?"

"They talked about cleaning up the basement."

They talk and talk and talk.

Blah, blah, blah.

I watch the traffic light turn from green to yellow to red.

I count the seconds between each color.

I watch the light turn from red back to green.

And then I tug at Mama's jacket.

"Can we go now?" I say.

"Hope to see you at the next meeting," says Mama.

"I'll be there," says Mr. Chan.

At last we're on our way again.

"Mama," I say, "you talk too much!"

"Celeste," says Mama, "you walk too fast!"

"You stop too much to talk and talk and talk," I say.

"Look!" says Mama.

I say, "Oh no!" It's Mrs. Castro. Here we go.

Blah, blah, blah.

Then I see Mrs. Castro is holding a long red leash
with a puppy at the other end.
"Can I stop to pet it?" I ask.
"I thought you were in a hurry!" says Mama.

But we stop and I kneel down and
the puppy licks my cheek.
Mrs. Castro tells me his name is Jake
and he's only ten weeks old and she
just bought him some toys.
She shows me the squeaky rubber
fire hydrant and the yellow rubber ball.

"Isn't he cute?" I say to Mama.

 Mama is laughing. "Talk, talk, talk," she says.

"Come visit Jake later," says Mrs. Castro.

"I have to get going."

"We have to go too," says Mama.

Then Mama and I are on our way again.

I slow down so I can walk with Mama.

We talk all the way to the supermarket.

We talk and talk and talk.

	DATE DUE		
OCT 2 4 2000			
NOV 2 2000			
FEB 15 2001			
MAR 25 2001			
APR 17 2001			